T0266714

"Barba inhabits the minds of children with an exactitude that seems to me so uncanny as to be almost sinister."—*The Guardian*

"Barba is intensely alive to the shifting, even Janus-faced nature of strong feeling."—*San Francisco Chronicle*

"*Such Small Hands* is a magnificently chilling antidote to society's reverence for ideas of infantile innocence and purity."—*Financial Times*

"Barba's stunning and beautiful prose helps us realize that our adult incomprehension is not absolute."
—*Los Angeles Review of Books*

"Each one of these pages is exquisite, and the end result is a perfectly expressed work that transmits the perverse and bizarre experience that is youth, where games signify life and death and where relationships are teased and pushed to the breaking point."—*Music & Literature*

"A lyrically rich and devastating portrayal of adolescent struggle."—*ZYZZYVA*

"A darkly evocative work about young girls, grief, and the unsettling, aching need to belong."— *Kirkus Reviews*

SUCH SMALL HANDS

Andrés Barba

Translated from the Spanish by
Lisa Dillman

With an afterword by
Edmund White

**TRANSIT
BOOKS**

Published by Transit Books
2301 Telegraph Avenue, Oakland, California 94612
www.transitbooks.org

Las manos pequeñas
Copyright © 2008 Andrés Barba
Originally published in Spanish by Editorial Anagrama S.A.
English Translation Copyright © 2017 Lisa Dillman
Afterword Copyright © 2017 Edmund White

First published in English by Transit Books in 2017

ISBN: 978-1-945492-00-6
LIBRARY OF CONGRESS CONTROL NUMBER: 2016961681

DESIGN & TYPESETTING
Justin Carder

DISTRIBUTED BY
Consortium Book Sales & Distribution | (800) 283-3572 | cbsd.com

PRINTED.IN THE UNITED STATES OF AMERICA

9 8 7 6 5 4

TABLE OF CONTENTS

SUCH
SMALL
HANDS

For Marina and Teresa, who were girls both
luminous and dark, like these.

And when the doll was so disfigured
that she no longer looked like a human baby,
only then did the girl begin to play with her.

ANONYMOUS, *A Woman in Berlin*

PART

ONE

HER FATHER DIED INSTANTLY, HER MOTHER IN THE HOSPITAL.

"Your father died instantly, your mother is in a coma" were the exact words, the first ones Marina heard. You could touch those words, rest your hand on each sinuous curve: expectant, incomprehensible words.

"Your father died instantly, your mother is in a coma."

Lips pronounce them without stopping. Quick, dry words. They come in thousands of different, unpredictable ways, sometimes unbidden. Suddenly they just fall, as if onto a field. Marina's learned to say them without sadness, like a name recited for strangers, like my name is Marina and I'm seven years old. "My father died instantly, my mother in the hospital."

Her mouth hardly moved and once she'd spoken, her lips were expressionless, the upper one jutting out slightly above the lower. Not making a face, though. Sometimes the words came slowly, rolling in from afar. As if they had chosen her, rather than she having chosen them. A strange homecoming, those words, a strange return to the things that made home. Fragrant. The words take on dimension, shooting upward and outward, making the air thick. Becoming something, becoming a thing. But a thing that's always veiled, and so she has to say:

"My father died instantly, and then my mother died in the hospital," and then make her way back through that thought to the other one, the real one, the slow one, the accident. Nothing as fragile as that surface. Nothing as slow or as fragile. First the sound of the road beneath the tires, the muffled, maritime sound of the road, the feel of the back seat, the danger at first almost imperceptible.

A second later it broke. What did? Logic. Like a melon dropped on the ground, split in one go. It started like a crack in the seat she sat on, its contact was no longer the same contact: the seatbelt had become severe. Before, long before the collision, was the smoothness of the seat she'd felt so many times, the upholstery with its fine white lines, which had somehow altered. Mamá's voice, to papá.

"Don't try to pass."

And that was the source of the fissure, the one that started in the seat, that included the quiet sound of the road beneath the tires as the car accelerated.

The impact was colossal.

The car jumped the meridian, flipped, and slid upside

down across the oncoming lane before smashing into the rocks just beyond the shoulder. And the whole accident, which Marina was unable to recall with any precision until four months later, was born of speed, sheer speed. There was nothing to be gleaned from it, nothing to unravel.

It was sound, too. A violent sound, but different from the one produced by the accident itself. A hollow, disjointed sound that erupted and then was immediately muffled in the distance, a sound that was not prolonged or sustained, and yet somehow accompanied the car as it flew over the meridian and flipped upside down.

The car falling, and where it fell, transforming. The car, making space for itself. That, more than ever, was when she had to fall back on the words. As if, of all the words that might describe the accident, those were the only ones that possessed the virtue of stating what could never be stated; or, as if they, of all words, were the only ones *there*, so close at hand, so easy to grasp, making what could never possibly be discerned somehow accessible. And after the sound, silence. Not the lack of sound, but silence. A silence that was neither a void nor a negation but a positive form, one that solidified what just a few instants ago had been elastic and supple: the metallic taste in her throat, her thirst.

Marina remembers thirst almost the second everything stopped. An unrelenting thirst that was part of the silence and the stillness, a thirst that couldn't be quenched even when she felt hands unbuckle her seatbelt, saw the face of that heavy, bleach-blonde woman, heard the other voice, the man.

"Don't touch her head; leave her like that, don't touch her head."

"Water," she said.

She said *water* the way you think of water when you learn that the human body is almost entirely made of it: an abstract water turned solid.

"Little girl. Are you okay? Can you hear me?"

The heavy woman with bleached hair was bending over her now, the bottle in her hand. Marina could see every single black root of the woman's hair, but nothing was taking root in Marina: not the liquid she was drinking, not the metallic taste of blood on her gums, not the heavy woman's roots; she felt like clay, as if everything inside her was soft, formless, slippery.

"Her head looks okay; it's her arm that's hurt."

Their muffled conversation filtered through to her. She felt a hand under her neck, slowly reaching under her back, another man, his hand was enormous, a hand that could have split her in two if it wanted, and yet was gentle.

"Respiratory tract's not obstructed."

"What's your name?"

"Marina."

"Marina, do you think you can move?"

"Yes."

"I want you to lie back on this stretcher."

When she was lifted she felt the pain for the first time.

An electric charge, searing through her entire torso and then subsiding, abating immediately, like her thirst. She couldn't move her left arm.

"What's that white stuff?"

"Those are your ribs."

And then when she sat up she saw the extent of the injury: the motionless arm, the raw flesh, the gaping flesh, sliced so cleanly that the skin fell away like a curtain, her ribs. She had to find a way to the words that would make it make sense, the words that were about to disappear.

"Marina, your father died instantly and your mother died just now."

They'd laid everything out beside her, ready for a panic attack, but the attack didn't come. Marina was still watching the words as if they were an airplane, flying from one end of the hospital room to the other; she was staring after the white contrail the words left in their wake. The girl doesn't erupt, doesn't cry, doesn't react. There were three people in white coats and black shoes: two women and a man. Three people with legs and arms and that unreal, almost magical quality that adults had always had for Marina; these ones in particular, though, were distinctly unmagical. Pause, wait for her to take in their words. But the girl doesn't cry, doesn't erupt, doesn't react. The girl still inhabits the suburbs of the words. Or perhaps it was just that creative thinking disassociated what it had no possible way of assimilating. The words were still polished and clean and superficial like the adults' black shoes.

"Do you understand what we're saying?"

"Yes."

"We're telling you that your parents are dead."

"Yes."

"Both of them."

"Yes."

You were supposed to say *yes*, keep repeating *yes*. A *yes* as polished and superficial as their shoes. Number and word: *yes*. Silence and sound: *yes*. Word detached from language, prior to language, forlorn, pure, limpid.

MARINA AWOKE with the vague feeling that there was something she had to do, that she had some obligation she hadn't met to the doctors who came to see her every morning and every afternoon. Maybe it was the obligation to be human, to cry and stamp her feet, to suffer. Over those two months of convalescence, Marina sank into their looks the way you sink into a tub. It was only right before the doctors came that she felt her parents' absence, but in such an abstract way that it never showed, like when you almost grasp a concept and then don't. She'd drop her hands onto the sheet, onto the picture of a house that the psychologist had made her draw, not because she was being dramatic but because letting her hands drop was a way of moving the throbbing pain in her arm to the paper, the house, the mountain and the tree, above the sun and the puffy-cotton cloud.

"You're really good at houses."

"No, I'm really good at trees."

"Will you teach me how to draw them?"

"First you make a fat trunk. Then three points. All brown. And then you do the leaves with light green."

"Like this?"

"Don't push down so hard. I've drawn tons of trees. That's why mine are so good."

"Look what I brought you: a doll," the psychologist said.

The doll was small and compact. The psychologist gave it to her to make her a real girl once and for all.

At first she was ecstatic. The doll, with her wide-open eyes, plastic eyes, heartrending eyes, eyes that opened and closed. To get them to close you had to lay her down and say, "Now you're going to go to sleep, aren't you, dolly? You're going to go to sleep because it's nighttime and you're very tired and you have to go to sleep, little dolly."

There, in bed: her.

Dolly repeated over and over, dolly always waiting to lift her arms and be picked up, and the past shrinking, loneliness shrinking. She had three fingers on each hand. And a light green dress. And a smiling, painted mouth. And legs that didn't bend. She navigated space like it was nothing, from the bed to the edge of the nightstand, from the cozy cavern of the bathroom to the boundless future of the window, always in Marina's hands, flying.

One day she said, "We have the same name: Marina."

Suddenly. As if it were a revelation.

"Your name's Marina."

And what if, like her, Marina started to have fewer memories, fewer and fewer memories, hardly any memories, no memories at all?

"We have the same name."

Because dolly was the only one who didn't lie. She was the only one calm, as if halfway through a long life. And she looked different from everyone else. Time passed over her, and she remained ever alert, like a visionary, astonished, lashless eyes (broken: now even when you laid her down, they didn't close).

"Now you're always awake, dolly; you're broken."

But she wasn't broken at all. Now what had never been visible became visible from up close: her skin. So real, that skin. Marina was entranced by the curve of her ear, her lip, the folds in the plastic, skin you could examine from up close, too close, too real to be true. She'd bring her face up to dolly's face, stick out her tongue, lick her eyes.

"Now you can see better."

And she could always see better. The past, the present, the future. What if Marina left dolly on the windowsill watching people walk by on the street for days in a row? She'd end up knowing everything there was to know and she'd grow and grow and the seams on her back would burst, like the scar on Marina's shoulder, and someone would have to come remove each one of her stitches with a pair of little black scissors.

The day she was supposed to be discharged from the hospital had almost arrived. The psychologist had told her a week ago, but she hadn't given her any additional information. She was leaving. Where was she going? She didn't know. To an island. To a mountain. To the sea. No, not to *the* sea, to *a* sea. Everything was *a*, a place that already existed. It wasn't so much the fear of leaving that terrified Marina but the idea of that space, that intricate, bountiful, preconceived place, full of beforehands.

One day she asked the psychologist.

"Where am I going to go?"

"To an orphanage."

But at that point the word held no meaning for Marina.

The doctors came to say goodbye, each in a white coat. All three of them told Marina how pretty she looked, all three smiling, puppet-like, marionettes in a hurry to leave quickly because they had so many important things to take care of. They'd stood there, asking her to raise her arm one more time, asking if it hurt when she held it this way, that way.

"You're going to live in a nice new house, a very pretty place with other girls, you'll see," the psychologist said.

"No parents?"

"No. But it's very pretty, you'll see."

Then a second later the psychologist was gone.

Marina peed in her pants. She felt the hot, acidic urine run down her legs to her shoes and she felt the shame, which was also hot: a dark, robust, inescapable mass. She cried, a slave to that hot shame. Marina's face, when the psychologist returned, was that of someone who'd been terrorized, and she wanted to calm her. She put her hand on her back, a hand with no conviction, like the words she'd just spoken, solemn as a newsflash.

"Here, I brought you some chocolate. Oh—did you have an accident?"

Saying yes was too humiliating, so she said nothing.

"Don't cry; come on, we'll get you changed."

But her shame did not subside with clean underwear. Her shame was elastic, something that swelled, like the maritime sound of the road beneath the wheels.

It was too hard to look forward to the orphanage; she didn't know how to do it. And unable to picture it, random images jumbled together and came gurgling out like a death rattle. She looked at dolly to quiet them. Someone had gone to her house and packed her a doubtful suitcase. Winter clothes and summer clothes all jumbled together.

Marina's cheeks burned when the car pulled up at the entrance.

"It's pretty, isn't it?"

And it was.

"Yes, it is."

But it was something else, too. It was haughty. It rose up with an odd pretension, as if superimposed over the playground was another playground, as if over the building someone had traced a very fine black line in the air that ran over the border of each of the windows and doors. The whole house looked like it was outlined against the landscape.

"It's enormous," the psychologist said.

The playground made Marina feel devotion in her stomach, and it felt nice, felt like intimacy. You couldn't put roots down in that devotion, but you could love it. The house made Marina feel afraid, as though the two of them—she and the house—were actually two people forced to live under the same cruel tyrant. A narrow, paved concrete path ran from the front gate to the orphanage door, its cement cracked by the plants and tree roots surrounding a black statue of Saint Anne.

At first glance, she looked soothing. Her arms were open in welcome: fine, maternal arms, though black and inescapable. You couldn't see her face until you got up close, and then she looked like a little girl, the childlike expression on her face refuted by how old and how black the sculpture was. A black, childlike, little old lady.

No one was there that day; the girls were on a field trip, not coming back until the following day. The principal wore a brown skirt and black shoes with gold buckles. Though her lips barely moved when she spoke, she gave the impression that she was always smiling.

"You're Marina, aren't you?"

"Yes."

"My name's Maribel. I'm the principal. You're very pretty, Marina."

And the word *pretty* sounded strange then, as if it had been split in two. And everything she said became part of the spell cast by that broken word: the dormitory, hallways, classroom, dining room, bathrooms, closets, the redhaired clown at the door with a chalkboard in his stomach on which someone had written: *Tomorrow, Field trip to Cola de Caballo* and tomorrow was now today, because the girls weren't there, because no one was there. Everything conspired to give that word back its meaning, and Marina had the urge to say that the dining room was *pretty* and so was the classroom, and the beds, all lined up in a row. That *pretty* was a giant hole swallowing everything up.

For dinner they had salad, three croquettes each, and a pear.

Meanwhile, the principal talked about classes, games, the other girls; she said their names as if reciting a memorized list. At that point the names were all empty, no girls inside them yet.

"I hear you're a very good girl," the director said at last, when they'd finished dinner.

And Marina felt happy, because she knew the meaning of that word. Its sound and texture were not alien to her.

And starting with that word she saw how her body reappeared, fiber by fiber, over the empty plates and the water jug that might break.

"I am; I'm good."

"Well, tonight you're going to go to bed early, because everybody's coming back tomorrow and you need to be rested."

The psychologist and the principal walked Marina up to the dormitory and quickly undressed her. Silently she got into bed.

"Do you know how to make yourself fall asleep?" the principal asked. "Count each breath, slowly, until the red light turns blue. . . ."

She was entranced by the wooden chests of drawers, by the girls' names written in colors on the drawers: Diana, Marcela, Julia, Sara, María, Ana, Mónica, Teresa, Raquel, Celia, Paloma, Irene.

She got out of bed and traced her fingers over the letters.

Would they write her name in colors like theirs, too, on another drawer: Marina?

She read them all as fast as she could. Dianamarcelajuliasaramaríaanamónicateresaraquelceliapalomairene.

PART

TWO

IT WAS ONCE A HAPPY CITY; we were once happy girls. They used to say: do this, do that, and we did it, we turned our hands, we drew, we laughed; they called us the faithful city, the enchanting city. We had proud eyes, strong hands. People thought we were just girls then.

We used to touch the fig tree in the garden and say, "This is the castle." And then we walked to the black sculpture and said, "This is the devil." And then we'd go back to the orphanage door and say, "This is the mountain." Those were the three things: castle, devil, mountain. That was the triangle you could play in.

And there was the hall mirror.

And our summer dresses.

And the night they changed our sheets and it felt so good to climb into fresh-smelling beds.

And the days we got *sanjacobos* for lunch: breaded fried ham and cheese.

It was as if we were all one mouth eating the ham, as if our cheese were all the same cheese: wholesome and creamy and tasting the same to all of us. The cheese was happiness. But then we had class after lunch, and it was long. And the time between lunch and class, and then between class and break time, passed slowly, suspended in the air.

When class was over we liked to play. We'd sing as the jump rope hit the sand with a dull crack. To get in the circle you had to pay attention, had to calculate the jump rope's arc, its speed, adapt your rhythm to the chorus. Once you were in you felt exposed, tense, as if each time the rope cracked down, it hit your mouth, or your stomach. With each thump you went around the world, instantly, quick as lightning; you had to make it. And hide-and-seek: you'd crouch behind a tree and then become part of the tree; if you didn't move you were invisible. You had to stay there, kneeling, feeling the coarse playground sand digging into your knees, leaving marks on your skin, until someone called your name, and then you had to run to base, where you were safe. What a strange word: safe.

One afternoon the adult said, "There's a new girl coming. Don't be scared."

But we weren't then. At first we weren't scared.

Before Marina ever arrived, first came speculation.

We didn't know any other way to love.

We went around preparing places, loving everything we could imagine, everything before our eyes. Some of us thought she'd be big, others said she'd be our size; some said she'd be very pretty, others didn't think so. Her first triumph was this: we were no longer all the same. We, who had been tamed, we, who made no distinctions among ourselves and our bodies, we, who all wanted the same things, were no longer all the same. Suddenly there were hands that we didn't recognize, and we became strangers. From one second to the next something had broken: our trust. It was as if, in a short space of time, we had all become aware of so many things, and they were sad, those things, so different from multiplication tables, from learning *c* from *k*, from our natural science book. Those things hurt, they flowed down like a river from upstairs, where the principal and the adults lived.

Why was there no more joy in this: "How much wood would a woodchuck chuck if a woodchuck could chuck wood? He would chuck, he would, as much as he could, and chuck as much wood as a woodchuck would if a woodchuck could chuck wood." There was no music to it anymore, no trees or woodchuck for us to imagine, teeth bared, just words like stones you couldn't find. Just a foretaste of Marina who now, yes, now we were afraid of.

Then one day, a day like any other day, she actually arrived.

We were on our way back from a field trip and the miracle was performed. There was nothing special about her.

The door opened and there was a girl, dark, pretty but not too pretty, with slack hands, shoes that weren't like ours, silhouetted in front of the statue of Saint Anne, almost as black as her, a shape that neither spoke nor smiled, with a doll in one hand and a stick in the other. So close, and like us, the same height.

"This is Marina," they said.

And yet she didn't look like us. She had dark-girl eyes. How could we describe her? How could we say, "This is what Marina was like the first time we saw her"? We might get tired, we might start to describe her and then have to keep going back to clarify things, and nothing we said would be right except for the feeling that you couldn't really see all the way inside that girl.

She was always on alert. Always.

Her eyes squinted when she was thinking, as if she herself disappeared into those slits and fed off her thoughts. And when she got up, she'd grope along, touching things, heavy, and yet seeming like she was about to take off and fly.

"I don't know what to do with that girl," the adult said.

And we didn't know what to do with our love, either; it was so heavy.

It would sneak up by surprise, just when it seemed like it wasn't coming back. Suddenly, in a flash, there it would be. We'd be copying a passage from a book and suddenly realize that our lines were all crooked, or that we'd skipped a word, or that we'd made an ink stain, or that we'd smeared the bottom of the page with our arms, or that we'd accidentally creased the paper. And Marina had been there watching over that mistake.

Everything around her was contaminated, and so were we.

But then at recess, out on the playground, everything went back again. Marina shrank and we grew. She stood alone, with her doll, by the statue of Saint Anne, watching us. Or was it the doll who was watching? We didn't know who the doll really was. Because sometimes she looked like Marina, and she, too, seemed to have a hungry heart, and clenched fists held close to her body, and she, too, was silent even when invited to join in; and she nodded her head back and forth, something we'd never seen a doll do before. And she seemed persecuted and excluded, too. If you sat her on the ground, from above she looked like a little girl and we were the adults, and we thought that we actually were a little like that, a tiny head you could hardly see, a head you had to lift by the chin in order to see its face. Even her face was like ours, though wary and full, like when you got scared.

"Her eyes are broken, that's why she can't close them. You have to lick her eyeballs so she can see or else she can't see."

Marina held out her doll; that was the first thing she'd said to us. We stuck our tongues out until the tips touched the cold glass of her eyes. And it was true: the doll could see then. Isn't that what an eye looks like when it can see? Open, blue, impenetrable. What if she started talking? That would scare the adults, but not us, we thought. A miniature life, easy to love. Suddenly everything came to us filtered through the doll, even innocence, because we were like her and she was like us. What good would it have done to say, "She's pretty, we like your doll"?

And it was all because Marina had come.

It was the same with our morning showers.

Before, we used to line up by the sinks. First we brushed our teeth. Then we took off our clothes and left them on the bench. Hot water and steam and shampoo, those things were happiness, too. And we used to play tricks all the time. Under the shower's jet it was different: we forgot each other and felt a little alone in our pleasure, as if we'd been abandoned. We felt a hand soaping up our backs and legs, but it was an invisible hand, because you had to close your eyes so you didn't get soap in them.

Who was the first one to notice it? We don't remember. We don't even know if we actually saw it: Marina's scar. We had to defend ourselves against that scar that Marina didn't hide. Suddenly we saw each other seeing it, we differentiated each other among things, among the others, we differentiated her, her back, her walk, her eyes, her face like a vague feeling of fear.

We didn't know sadness until we had a point of comparison.

And it all started there, like a breach, in her scar.

We became aware of each other and we felt naked before that body that wasn't like our bodies. For the first time we felt fat, or ugly; we realized that we had bodies and that those bodies could not be changed. Just as she had materialized, we materialized: these hands, these legs. Now we knew that we were inescapably the way we were. It was a discovery you could do nothing with, a discovery that served no purpose. We huddled together when she approached. We were afraid to touch her.

"What's the matter with you?" the adult asked.

But she was staring at us and she was so close; it was like she were saying, "It's my secret. All mine."

"Would you mind telling me what on earth is the matter with all of you today?" they asked.

But Marina didn't react, didn't get involved. She stood there, patient. She closed her eyes when she was told to, and we watched the shampoo bubbles being rinsed from her hair, sliding down her body to her feet; and the swirl they made in the drain, we saw that, too, and the towel they used to dry her with.

ONE OF THE FIRST THINGS Marina discovered was this: their shoes were all the same. Black, round-toed shoes. All of their faces too dark, too tanned and hardened by the sun. All of their dresses too bright.

Sunlight and air filtered through the girls' dresses and their hands, and they held onto their toys too tight. They'd been stripped of something childlike and yet their faces were childlike, it was as if their bodies had developed too early, before their faces, or their faces too late, a step behind their bodies.

Maybe that's why it was so hard to tell them apart.

Marina started at their shoes and worked her way up. The higher she looked the more differences she discerned: fatter knees, skinnier legs. But when she got to their faces she had the impression she'd made a mistake along the

way, that the legs she'd started at didn't belong to the face
she'd ended up at but to another, darker one, a face that
never actually materialized yet whose presence she could
perceive: a common face.

What difference did it make that one of them walked
over and said her name was Diana? Couldn't she just as
easily have been Sara or Julia or Marcela? It was miracu-
lous that they moved at all. When she thought of them
they seemed permanently still, stunned. Maybe later,
when Marina stopped looking and crouched down to
her doll, they changed, differentiated themselves; there
was no way to know. In class they sat with their backs to
her and in her mind she pictured the arm of one leading
to the head of another, jumping from their feet to their
skirts, through their fingers. The imaginary figure stood
still a second and then faded away. And then suddenly it
was night and they went to dinner.

They were different when they were sleeping.

All together, they looked like a team of sleepy little
horses. Something in their faces slackened, became
friendly. They slept with an unbearable patience. When
they were asleep they were like an oil painting, they gave
Marina the impression that different faces rose up from
beneath their faces, faces that bore no resemblance to
their daytime faces: peculiar, polished faces. They had
a defiant, challenging quality about them despite being
at rest, like dozing predators. If she looked closely, Marina could see the pulse on their necks, could smell their

sleep smell, different from their daytime smell, more sickly sweet, or maybe just a little more intense. Some of them got tiny little folds, miniscule creases by their mouths, invisible gills that made them seem like sea creatures that only came out at night.

Why were they beautiful then?

She didn't know. Marina was fixated on the ellipsis of the girls' sleeping faces. She couldn't wait for night, pretending to fall asleep immediately and then waiting until they were breathing deeply. Then she'd count to fifty, and when she was sure they were asleep she'd sit up slightly to see them better. The slightest sound startled her and she'd lie back down in bed, closing her eyes and counting to fifty once more.

Sometimes she'd sit up and nothing moved; silence floated over the dormitory. She'd slip out of bed feeling the cold floor tiles beneath her feet and creep over to one of them. She'd get so close her lips would brush against her. She'd think, "If she woke up now she'd see me," and that thought frightened her. She'd rest her head very carefully on the pillow, inhaling the girl's breath.

Just like pain. Exactly like pain.

The orphanage psychologist dwelled on it obsessively. She'd ask her to describe inkblots, make her draw things, and then suddenly ask about her parents and the accident.

The accident.

"My father died instantly, my mother in the hospital."

It was like leaning over one of the sleeping girls' sweet-smelling, inscrutable faces. She could get as far as, "This one has a small nose, that one has thicker lips than the other, and this one breathes differently; this one rests her arms on her chest and that one lays them at her sides like a corpse; and there's one who never closes her eyes all the way and that's her way of sleeping."

"Tell me what you remember."

"I remember the upholstery. It was dark, with fine white lines."

"Describe the upholstery."

"Black, dark blue, almost black. And scratchy."

The enumeration of details satisfied the psychologist. The deliberate, meticulous, polished enumeration. Marina made an effort to recall even the most circumstantial details, colors and shapes, words the psychologist jotted down anxiously in a black notebook. Whenever her memory failed her, she'd just invent a color and slot it between true things. That seemed to change the scene, to turn her memories into things that were solid, things you could take out of your pocket and put on the table. Was the psychologist writing, or drawing? Was she maybe drawing one of the girls' faces? Yes, that was it: a sleeping-girl face.

"What else do you remember?"

"There was sand on the floor of the car, just a little, a little pile of sand, and I was watching it and thinking it was going to move when we went around the curve."

"And did it move?"

"No."

Then back to the same, always the same.

"My father died instantly and then my mother died in the hospital."

But the cadence of the words had changed now. They were like an accusation, a shameful secret, something that flowered just below the skin's surface, like a swamp plant; now the words were moist, and they grew. The other girls' existence made it impossible for her to inhabit the suburbs of the words. When she was dreaming the words she felt like they spent their time there, above her face, and that they were as old as a building, as the furniture.

"And what else?"

"The lines were very thin, and then they got thick."

"How could that be?"

"They did, they got thick. And the seat wasn't scratchy anymore; it got soft. And I thought that after a while my feet were going to touch the floor and then I'd be able to move the little pile of sand with my toe."

That was about the time that caterpillars started appearing in the playground. You had to be careful because they stung, the adult said. You'd see them parading majestically, covered in very fine hair like little mink coats, always single file. Marina wondered how a caterpillar's body worked, what the springs and levers looked like that made it arch like that, so that every time it moved it was like a shiver passing through its body.

"Then I felt a shiver go through my whole body. It started in my head and went all the way to my feet."

"Before the accident?"

"Yes."

They always headed for the trees and then climbed their way up. Caterpillars wore masks, too. If you looked at them up close their faces were old and black and wrinkled, like the statue, and they looked like they were going faster than they really were. It made her dizzy to think that they were dangerous, that they stung. Marina picked up a stick. She thought of a number: four. She started counting from the head of the procession. One. Two. Three. Four. And the fourth one she jabbed with the stick. The caterpillar recoiled, as if it had received an electric shock, and a dark liquid bled out. Marina was transfixed, unable to pull the stick out. The rest of the procession froze, too, immediately. Marina salivated. What movement, what contact, what inaudible sound had been communicated to them, "Number four just died"? How had the news traveled from one to the next? It was strange: they stopped entirely.

"And then everything stopped."

"After the accident, you mean?"

"Yes, after, right after."

"Everything?"

"Everything. And I thought if I sat still, everything would turn to stone and I would turn to stone, too."

"And what happened?"

The circle happened. Their being frozen wasn't real. Slowly, the other caterpillars began to bob, looking like they were turning towards the center, where they had to bow, and the fourth caterpillar was the center. Marina realized then that she wasn't alone, that the other girls had gathered around her. The fourth caterpillar was still moving. Was it asking for something? Which of the surrounding caterpillars had it loved the most? The procession's activity hadn't come to a close, just as the circle of girls surrounding Marina had not closed. She could feel their breath, their bodies pressing against her back, a girl's head peering over her shoulder. If she turned now, she'd kiss her accidentally.

"Everything stopped moving, and we all turned to stone and I felt how my hands and my eyes and my legs were all stone, and everything around me was stone, even the car was stone, and there was a wizard who turned us all to stone."

"A wizard?"

"Yes."

But the girls' breathing made it impossible to lose herself in that illusion. Marina didn't pull the stick out until the fourth caterpillar stopped moving completely, and when she did they saw that she'd split it in two, that the fourth caterpillar was now two caterpillars. The circle was closing in. The procession, too. A notion was traveling from one to the next, a message being passed through their skin, through the almost transparent fibers on their necks. Maybe the caterpillars were deliberating before the cadaver, mourning the fourth caterpillar, trying to convince the dead one that they weren't callously abandoning it.

"And what did the wizard look like?"

"Oh, I didn't see him."

"Well, then how do you know he was a wizard?"

Marina now felt she was surrounded by mouths, felt that each girl was a mouth and each mouth filled with fangs. And each fang was hard. The other caterpillars crowded in so close to the fourth caterpillar that they almost covered it completely. From where the girls stood, from their shocked expressions, it looked as if the procession had decided to devour the fourth caterpillar, as if the living were suddenly possessed by a violent covetousness of the dead one's peace. What was it? Whatever it was, for a second something fierce had flashed in each of the living caterpillars' eyes. Marina felt the unmistakable presence of the girls' bodies above her. The circle had closed ranks.

She tried to escape. Petrified, she was convinced they were trying to block her way, forcing her to lean in over the circle with them. The girls' words reached her, muffled. Humiliated, she assumed they were taking revenge on her for spying on them at night. She panicked, pushing them frantically, feeling the wall of flesh close in and grow solid.

"I know he was a wizard because it's always a wizard, because only wizards can turn things to stone."

"But you didn't see him."

43

"Well, I saw him a little."

"And what did he look like?"

"He was big and black, like the statue."

The girls' solid mass was big and black, like the statue. Now that she was closed in, trapped in the caterpillars' circle, now that they wouldn't let her go, she felt the closeness of their faces for the first time, much closer than at night when she spied on them. The olive tone of their skin. Seen in the light of day, they had tiny black spots by their eyes and mouths, like the black spots on the caterpillars' faces. Marina stopped shoving and drew back as much as she could. She closed her eyes. The girls talked about the caterpillars, picked the stick up off the ground, poked it at each other, examined the blood of the fourth caterpillar as if trying to solve a mystery. Her only thought was this: "Don't let them touch me."

Then, slowly, they filtered away.

They dropped the stick by the tree and almost immediately she heard their voices on the other side of the playground, jumping rope once more, shouting. When Marina opened her eyes, the caterpillar procession, too, began to fall back. Slowly they surrounded the shattered beauty of the fourth caterpillar and then began their majestic ascent towards the fig tree once more. If she were their size, she'd see the fig tree the way they did: a rutted, mammoth precipice.

But they hadn't all left. One of the girls had stayed behind, was still there beside her. To Marina she looked like the survivor of a catastrophe; she couldn't tell if her face registered joy or sorrow.

"Are you the one who killed the caterpillar?" she asked.

"Yes," Marina said.

From up close she looked the same as the other girls. Everything about her was anonymous. The girl leaned over and picked the stick up off the ground, examined it carefully, held it out to Marina.

"Did you kill it with this stick?"

"Yes."

"Why?"

"I just thought of a number. I said, 'Four.' And then I counted to four and I killed the fourth one."

Now that the two of them were together, it was as though the caterpillar were dying all over again, just for them. It was too devout to be a common carcass, still enshrouded by the crawling community that had abandoned it; the black liquid that had bled out turned almost clear.

"Should we bury it?" Marina asked.

"Okay."

They sat down together and began to dig. Every once in a while their hands touched, and they flinched, as if suspecting how brutal love can be, as if aware of the viciousness of its physical expression and afraid to sense it in the touch of their hands as they dug a tiny grave for the caterpillar. Maybe the beginning was no more than that: something that brought them together. With their eyes open, they pitied the caterpillar more, wanted to make it a pretty grave, a grave to express everything the caterpillar had been: the fourth in the procession, the favorite of another caterpillar who was now mourning.

"My father died in the accident and then my mother died in the hospital," Marina blurted out. She wanted to feel closer to the girl, and to the caterpillar. The girl turned and looked towards the orphanage door.

All that was black and full of grace: the statue.

The girl stiffened. Marina had hurled the words like stones off a cliff. Now she was waiting to hear them drop, to judge their depth. But the stones didn't hit bottom, they just kept falling, into a void.

The stones were suspended.

And slowly, as if she'd fallen asleep there, it got late. And they had to go back to class.

THE BUILDING HAD GONE DARK, but we hadn't. Not yet. They put movies on for us at night and we were still happy then; we lived them so intensely that sometimes we cried and got scared and the adult had to come and tell us that it wasn't real, that it was just a movie, and so our feelings couldn't be real either.

Slowly, for no apparent reason, we started to wonder: "What about Marina?"

Marina never got worked up. We watched her out of the corner of our eye. "What about Marina?"

We shivered and the cold seemed to come from her; and when we opened our eyes up we realized that we'd actually been thinking, and that it was Marina who was our thought. And just as the movie was over, Marina was over.

After the movies we always talked; we told each other which parts we'd liked and which parts we hadn't, and talking was an act of love, something that united us, because it kept the movie alive. Recollecting was almost like watching it again, there, vibrant, the pleasure almost throbbing.

"What did you think, Marina, did you like it?"

"Well, I already saw it in the theater, so I already knew who the bad guy was and I didn't like it as much, because you never like a movie as much the second time."

And we didn't know what to do with that. It was as if Marina had already seen all movies, already gone on all field trips, already played all games; there was something terrible in her past. She'd already lived so many things. She buried her head in the pillow and saw everything, she rested her head and it was heavy as a rock, filled with memories, she pressed down on her pencil (How many pencils had she had? Thousands? Millions?) and even the pencil was a little envious, wishing she would use it to write all those things that Marina had already lived.

"So tonight when I saw it I knew right from the very beginning who the bad guy was; I said, 'That's the bad guy,' and it wasn't the same as the first time."

We'd been happy until Marina showed up with her past. We held it in then. But later, when we went out to play, we didn't know what to do with that thought; we were plagued by a feeling of rage and surprise, and we wanted to gnaw away at her, little by little.

"Hey, Marina, come here," we said.

And when she did, we pulled her hair. Nausea made us salivate and the saliva was like blood: how easy it was to humiliate. But she had humiliated us, too. She was so serene when she approached; she was happy. So without a word we pulled her hair. Maybe Marina had already had her hair pulled, too, but not the way we did it.

"And then, one summer, we went to the beach, and I had a ton of friends there, and one day we went out on a boat."

Feeling her hair yanked again, her face screwed up, a strangled echo flashed across her face. Like prey with its mouth open. And then she kept walking, moving in the shadows like a vampire; now she was afraid to remember and hunched down into herself a little and made a little-girl face, and at recess she started wandering off on her own. She'd lie on the ground and braid grass.

We loved her furtively then. Her eyes smiled sadly, the house relaxed, and we had to be very still and wait, to watch her again. It was a little like falling in love with her, with her body, with her memories. She couldn't understand our love. She could only consent, that was all; if we went to her, she could nod her head and accept her happy fear because we were finally there, and there were so many of us, and we held our hand out to her. The ball was round and bumpy. A dark brown, flat Adidas basketball that hardly bounced, its letters worn. Mystery girl, mystery girl bouncing the ball very hard and moving toward the basket, and us shouting:

"Here!"

She turned and passed the ball forcefully, body tense, thin legs, sweat on her temples. It was all so easy when we were playing basketball. We'd go in tired, enter a place full of emotions, a deep space; the ball bounced against the rim three times and then, very slowly, did not go in, and we had to shout, "Oh!" as loud as possible, feeling it swell up from our stomach, because Marina was there, and she'd shot and almost made a basket. It was ten-twelve. Marina became a little more coarse, a little less serious and pretty, and her laughter when the ball didn't go in was both gleeful and frightened. Was it her, or us? Were we forgiving her? Was that what love was? That desire to watch her play forever, play until the end of time, an eternal tie, or maybe almost always a tie, to make it more exciting. But then the game would end and we'd have to go back to class. In the time between laughing and eating, we grew serious again; we traced Mickey Mouse drawings against the window because it was easier that way, and Marina's always came out the best, it was almost like the real Mickey Mouse, like hers was actually full of time, of memories, of things she'd seen and touched. A new Mickey Mouse that bore no resemblance to ours.

"Once I went to Disneyland Paris."

Suppressed secret of Disneyland Paris. Suppressed secret a thousand times repeated, taken for granted in the hands and eyes of Marina, going to Disneyland Paris. Again, the rumble of dull thunder off in the distance, the thunder of her life without us. We wanted her to tell us about it but didn't want to ask.

"I got my picture taken with the real Mickey Mouse, and there was a huge castle, and then I got a Mickey Mouse notebook, and some Mickey Mouse pencils, and an eraser that smelled like strawberries when you squeezed it."

She couldn't see that the memory was too delicate for us; we didn't know how to grasp it. Those castles, that colored glass, the balconies Mickey and Minnie stood on, none of that could ever be ours. We ambled awkwardly alongside Marina's memory, always parallel, always tired, always hungry, but the urgency of our desire wasn't enough to bring it to life and then we tired of trying, and desire turned to rage against that girl who seemed too old.

"What do we care about Mickey Mouse and Disneyland and your stupid vacation?"

We stuck our tongue out at her.

"And there was a roller coaster, and I went on it three times."

If the adult wasn't watching, we hit her. Never very hard, usually just softly. She'd crouch down to pick something up and we'd stab her butt with a sharp pencil. She'd flinch and we'd laugh. Like a glass, her face filled up with humiliation. So full of thoughts we couldn't guess, so proud. Warm and dark, her eyes filled with tears she

never cried, she'd yank at her dress and pull it hard, as
if she were trying to stay here with us and not go back,
not return to Disneyland Paris, to her vacation, to the
roller coaster, as if keeping her memories and deciding
not to share them ever again, domesticating her anger.
Then she'd go back to her doll, that hateful doll—and she
loved it—she'd stay away from us at recess with her doll
in her hand and she'd love the doll. She'd go home, to her
memories. Did she tell the doll what she remembered?
Maybe. She talked to her, and we felt her hanging around
our neck, that tiny little thing that was Marina's doll, that
thing she loved instead of loving us.

"Don't you want to play basketball?"

"No."

"Go to hell."

But that's not what we meant. What we meant was: tell
us about your trip to Disneyland Paris again, and about
how you got your picture taken with Mickey Mouse; tell
us about the roller coaster and what it feels like when
you go down the hill, and how you got a notebook and
an eraser that smelled like strawberry, tell us if it seems
strange or if it's just normal, and if you want to eat the
strawberry-smelling eraser, if you crave it, tell us about
holding the real Mickey Mouse's hand when you got your
picture taken with him and how you think it's the real
Mickey Mouse, who any minute now is going to go off
with Minnie because the two of them live in that castle,

and it's real because it's right there and it has doors and windows you can touch.

"No."

We suffered her anger like a curse; it was cast on us suddenly. The curse of an evil, resentful witch. Maybe the evil witch loved us, too, and just didn't know what to do with her love, and wandered off crying; maybe beneath her hatred, too, was a little orchestra singing its love and suffocating her; and maybe she saw the darkness of her love as if from the window of a train. Poor evil witch, poor lovesick evil witch.

"And the evil witch's castle was at Disneyland Paris, too."

Tell us about it again, and tell us about how you had parents, and a room of your own, and a wall with a poster of Alice in Wonderland. Without understanding, she just stared at us and asked:

"Why?"

Then she stood back and dark red shadows covered her shoulder. Saving herself for the doll, she'd wander off again, to the black statue. "It's my secret, all mine." When we leaned over her we wanted to kiss her hair; it didn't smell like ours smelled, and that was something you couldn't fake. Tell us about how you were driving along with them when they died. Her eyes were open. It was a hard, shiny memory, like the crickets we heard outside when we went to bed. Tell us.

"No."

"Go to hell."

But of that violence was born a dark, gurgling pleasure, the supple feeling of having won, or being on the
verge of winning.

One Wednesday night we stole Marina's doll without
her realizing, and she woke up in a panic. Now she was
unprotected, like us. Now she tried to love, and her hun-
ger had no object. For a minute we thought she was going
to tell on us, but she didn't. She could hardly even move.

"Give her back, give me my doll back," she said.

So we gave her a leg. We broke it off.

"Here."

And we wanted to say: this is so you'll look at us. It
was easy to love her again then. Love was ancient, the
way things had always been, even. She threw the doll's leg
down by the tree and forgot about it. But we wanted to
know what it felt like; what was left, between the doll's leg
and the whole doll, and what was missing now. Something
inside Marina had gone slack, as if she'd lost her strength.
Now she'd come to us, we thought.

And so the broken head, and the rest of it—the body,
the arms, the remaining leg—we took it all and buried it
in the playground, with the dead caterpillar.

THIS IS THE MOMENT when Marina realizes something: *I'm different.* And as always, the realization itself outshines the symbolic event that led to it, the realization emerges from the sludge of reality preformed, round and irrefutable, something that had always been there: I'm different.

Marina insists on fingering the realization constantly, the way a newborn touches its body to prove that it's there. What if the realization suddenly grew so big that Marina was overwhelmed by it? Then she'd have to impose it on the girls. There would be no more day. There would be no more night. She would have to become what providence, through that realization, had imposed on her. It was like carrying everything she knew with her at all times, like carrying something haughty and cruel, like a flag. *I'm different.*

Faith in that belief, even just for a moment, is all it takes for everything to change.

Delivered from fear by the realization, now all she wants is to prove it, so when they go back to class, back to their language lesson, she is the only one who seems happy; she raises her hand every time the teacher asks a question, even if she doesn't know the answer. She wants to make clear that she's come to a realization, but doesn't know how to do it. She'd have liked not to have to show it, have liked to be able to will the girls to sense her realization, and for it to make them all turn and gaze at her in amazement, as if she were a dazzling vision.

So when they go to the cafeteria and lunch is served, she knows exactly what she has to do. It's as though she can feel the scar on her shoulder once more, as though the scar is sovereign and burning her, like a sign engraved into her. Exactly like that.

They're having soup and cheese omelets for lunch.

The girls stare longingly at the food. They're sad and food momentarily frees them from contemplation, that's why they pounce on it. One girl has a noodle stuck to her face, by her mouth; a tiny white noodle, like a headless little worm, sleeping there. Marina stares at that noodle as if it were a slow plague, stares at the mouth opening and closing as the girl spoons in more soup. She has just realized that the mouth is a hole, that things can be introduced through it. If she could explain what she saw, she would say it all starts with that girl's mouth-hole with the noodle stuck to it, that everything begins right there; on that dark mouth that won't stop opening and closing.

Suddenly Marina thinks: "I'm going to stop eating."

The hole made her feel sick even though the food smells good, even though the springy, golden omelet awaits.

I'm going to stop eating.

"Marina, aren't you going to eat?"

"No."

The adult's voice: measured, reasonable.

"Aren't you hungry?"

"No."

The girl looks up at the adult slowly.

She no longer wants to be like her, to look like her.

Time passes and only her thought remains.

The other girls finish eating and trickle out of the cafeteria. All through lunch Marina remained impassive, didn't touch her food, and with each passing moment her prestige grew. A solemn prestige, a city within a city: Marina's not eating. The news traveled through their skin, through the contact of their elbows at the table. Maybe in some remote past there existed another mythical heroine who once attempted what Marina is now attempting but didn't make it. That sinister decision, sealed tight like an almond: I'm going to stop eating.

When Marina is left alone she sees that from time to time an anonymous head appears, peeking through the crack in the window overlooking the playground, and she knows then that the mystery has been established.

"Just have one spoonful of soup and your omelet."

"I don't want any."

Sometimes two heads, impossible to recognize.

They look in, and then immediately disappear. And that spying is the girls' first real act of love for Marina. She savors it like a delicacy; now she has to be true to that act of love. Like always, like every act of love, there is something urgent and coercive about it, something that forces her to hold to the decision to defend the love she inspired. If that act were never-ending, infinitely drawn out, Marina would go through what lovers sometimes do: she would become a slave more to the act itself than to the driving force behind it; she would be trapped by the act, would see nothing but the act and be forced to repeat it obsessively.

"Just three bites of omelet and the fruit."

"No."

"Aren't you hungry, though?"

"No."

The adult and the girl are not really talking, they're whispering; the realization is fresh and they're both still feeling a little faint.

"Fine. Don't eat. You'll have dinner tonight. Go on, then. Go."

When she goes out to the playground the girls stop playing and turn toward her. Now that Marina has triumphed there is no reason to delay fear, or contact.

Marina walks over to them and smiles. The girls, however, stand rooted in their solemnity.

Marina didn't eat dinner that night, didn't have breakfast the next morning, either. At lunch she'd gone exactly one day without eating. Although the adults had grown increasingly insistent at each meal, Marina had not relented. And at each meal, she left the cafeteria a little later, a little more tired. Each victory was decisive. There was something majestic and tough in Marina's pallor when she made her way from the cafeteria, a sort of ritual mask, a repository of strength the other girls found inconceivable. If the adults had all exited the orphanage at that moment and left them alone when Marina emerged, they might have knelt down right there on the playground and worshipped her.

Her expression had changed, too; she looked more like a lynx now, like a cat. Her movements were feline, maybe because she was weak. Her steps were spaced out, but had a sort of nervous spring at the end that made her look tense, taut. Even her eyes seemed to have changed color. They looked both challenging and inscrutable, as if the battle were only being waged inside her, as if she were absolutely indifferent to everything going on around her.

At recess on the day after Marina decided to stop eating, the girls were jumping rope on the other side of the playground. It was as if they'd caged her over in the opposite corner; they wanted her calm. And although she was, she'd never been as threatening as she was then. One of the girls broke away from the group and approached her timidly. She did it so slowly, her steps so apprehensive, that she didn't realize she was trying to approach her until she was almost beside her already. Even if she didn't pay any attention to her, she'd still be there, trying to get closer. What was her name? She still didn't have it. Finally they looked at each other.

"Come here," Marina said.

The girl stood expectantly, open, not knowing what to say. She came, fearful. The thought of being touched by that girl made Marina tremble. "Come here."

The girl came. If she'd reached out her hand, she could have touched her face.

"We have to hide," she told her.

"Why?"

"Because I want to show you something."

The grass behind the fig tree was still damp from the rainfall the night before. It smelled of moist earth, of rot. Marina unbuttoned her shirt, pulled it down off of her shoulder. They sat down together on the damp earth. Nothing brings two people closer than being scared together. Her scar had faded, too, like a blemish. The stitches' tiny indentations had disappeared almost entirely; now there was just a curved, raised bump running from her shoulder to her sternum. The dazzling seduction of the scar. It was still cold and cloudy out. The skin around the scar contracted in a fleeting spasm and the girl opened her mouth, as if she wanted to devour everything: the air, the feel of the fig tree, Marina's arrogance, her own fear. It wasn't the same scar she saw in the bathroom every day when they took their showers; this one was crying out to be touched, to be admired, nothing made it hide now.

"I got this in the accident."

"Oh."

"And there was this white stuff you could see and it was my ribs. And then they picked me up by my shoulders and put me in an ambulance."

"Why aren't you eating?" the girl asked.

"I don't know."

Now there was no refuge. The cold air took her breath away, made her hope wane. Marina didn't want this conversation, she wanted to be touched but didn't know how to communicate her desire.

"Before you could see the stitches but now you can't see them anymore."

The girl turned back to the scar again. Her gaze was lost in its abyss. Marina felt the weakness of her own blood; she hadn't eaten in thirty hours and was lightheaded; she felt like she was going to fly. For a second the girl's face turned white, bluish, like an overexposed photo. Was her face going to disappear, too?

"Then the stitches disappeared and then it turned like this."

"Like what?"

"Like this, with no stitches, now you can only see the

skin and the scar, like a little worm, like when you take a cloth and fold it over."

Marina scooted closer. So close she could almost feel her contact, the warmth of her body. She stared at her hands; the girl bit her fingernails. Some of them were dirty, as though she'd been digging in the dirt. She wanted that hand on her, wanted it to touch her. She wanted it like something impossible, like heaven itself was contained in that hand and she longed for it to swoop down onto her.

"Before I never wanted anyone to touch me there be-cause it gave me the chills, but now I do, and sometimes I touch it too and I can't feel my skin, it's like having a piece of paper on your skin and what you're touching is just the paper."

She angled towards her more, feeling the girl with-draw, tense, brusque.

"You can't feel it?"

"No. Well, only a little."

Desire passed through the girl, too. Like stagnant wa-ter that suddenly begins to drain, imperceptibly.

And devotion mixed in with the desire.

"Do you want to touch it?"

"Yes."

But the girl didn't react right away. After saying *yes* she sat still for a few moments, not moving. She looked up. Marina felt as if they were surrounded by people, as if the ground was full of heads, right there in front of them.

They swayed all together now, an ocean of heads, of penetrating, unblinking eyes. It seemed they'd been there for a month, sitting there, just like that, unmoving.

"Touch it."

The girl reached out her hand.

"Touch it."

She felt like she was going to faint, she dreamed that her neck tensed and her head shot up. Her neck was elastic; her head stretched up, above the fig tree, above the house, the statue. Her jaw contracted, her tongue stuck out.

"Why are you sticking out your tongue?"

Her arms jerked. She tried to get up but her head was so heavy it felt like there was a weight on top of it. Now she'd have that weight pressing down on her forever, that weight that made her head wag back and forth, made heat surge up her back and then turn freezing cold; she dropped to her side, feeling the damp pleasure of the ground, of her own exhaustion.

"Touch me," she whispered.

But the girl ran away. She heard her steps grow fainter as she rushed off across the playground, and a moment later the sound was barely audible. The voices of the other girls playing still echoed off in the distance, but their song was no longer the one they sang to the rhythm of the jump rope, it accelerated like a crazy dance, their voices shriller, more piercing, almost inhuman.

She lost consciousness.

The adult panicked when she saw her there beside the fig tree, skirt hiked up to her waist, shirt unbuttoned, legs splayed. She looked as if she'd been rattled back and forth for hours and then dropped, a beautiful disjointed dance step frozen in time, isolated in space; an impossible, infantile, scandalous-yet-spirited dance step, a dance step of unimaginable strength for a body so small. She was kneeling, face to the ground, her skirt folded up above her slender legs. Her toes pointed in, like a baby, so defeated, so devoid of humanity that the adult felt a wave of repulsion.

The two adults carried her to the infirmary like a bride with a train of silent girls trailing behind. They put her to bed and covered her up. The doctor diagnosed a slight case of anemia and told them she had to be fed immediately.

PART
THREE

EVERYTHING WAS DIFFERENT at the zoo. It all started at the zoo: the smell of the zoo, the nervous excitability as we stepped off the minibus.

All that was new: the zoo. All that was violent: the zoo.

And the idea that the whole world is contained in one fang, and that that fang can be seen in its mouth, and it's white, and made to sink into flesh, and that the wolf, who is bad in real life, looks good when he's in his cage. Then you sense how they were made for each other, the wolf and the cage, how the wolf has been tamed and his fur has turned yellow in the shade, how the forest is contained in his eyes. We were allowed to put our hand almost up to the railing, so we'd be scared and say:

"What if there were no bars? Can you imagine?"

The wolf seemed hear us, to understand our words;

it raised its snout and gave us a look full of saliva and wanted to pounce on us.

And the elephants? And the rhinoceroses? And the seals? No, the seals were predictable and silly, nosing the ball around and getting rewarded with little fish; but the elephant was tired of its peanuts and had thick skin, and we had to shout at it for it to even turn and notice us. Then it looked up, exhausted, and drank listlessly from a dirty trough, lumbering heavily, as if each movement were bothersome, each step a tremendous effort, a fight it never won; and we pitied the elephant more than the seal, because it was bigger, and sadder, and more like us.

Marina was uneasy. She had been all morning, since we got up and took our showers. Then, at the peacocks, she stood there transfixed. We were near her and could sense her uneasiness. But at the same time it was as if her uneasiness transformed her, made her radiant and luminous.

"What are you looking at, Marina?"

"The peacocks. They're so pretty, the peacocks."

"They are."

"They're pretty but they're not, the way they look around like that, with a thousand eyes on their tails."

Inexplicably, we all edged closer, without meaning to. An inevitable attraction made us crave contact with her, seek out her voice, yearn for her to look at us. We no longer cared about the animals, or felt scared of the wolf, or sorry for the elephant, or admired the glimmering grace of the dolphins; we wanted Marina's contact, and we didn't know how to cast ourselves into that desert.

We wanted to ask, "Where are you, Marina?"

And yet she was right there beside us, overflowing, gazing at the peacocks; we knew she was going to speak to us, and we longed for her word. If she'd said, "Surrender now; throw yourselves to the wolf," we would have done it. If she'd said, "Jump on that peacock and kill it," we'd have done that, too.

"Tonight we're going to play a game," she said.

"What game, Marina?"

"Just a game I know."

"How do you play?"

"I'll tell you tonight."

"Can't you tell us now?"

"No. Tonight."

So the rest of the trip was tinged with the anxiety of the wait. The wait was essential. And at lunch we watched them feed the tigers and saw that they, too, were anxious when one man entered from one side while another one distracted them from the other and put down enormous slabs of raw meat for them. Behind the cage, as the man was leaving, something cracked, and the tigers fell instantly upon the meat. There were three of them. They coiled around like ivy, their backbones coming together at a single lump of flesh and fury so that they resembled a make-believe, three-headed creature, devouring the meat. Their snouts covered in blood. They had told us tigers were beautiful; they lied to us.

On the bus back we tried to sing songs, but we couldn't stop picturing the tigers' snouts, the wolf's fangs, the elephant's smell, the dolphin's plasticky skin, the monkey's neglect, wanting to be human and not succeeding.

Minne Minnehaha went to see her Papa,
Papa died, Minne cried,
Minne had a newborn baby,
Stuck it in the bathtub to see if it could swim.

"How does the game go, Marina?"

"I'll tell you tonight."

It was night now. We were in bed; the lights had been turned out. With the lights out we all looked surprisingly alike. The game hung over us before we began. Anxious for the game. A secret told twenty times under the covers, fingers crossed: the mystery of the game and the joy of the game as we waited, arms crossed, holding our breath.

"Everybody come here."

"Where, Marina?"

"Here, to my bed."

How did our desire begin? We don't know. Everything was silent in our desire, like acrobats in motion, like tightrope walkers. Desire was a big knife and we were the handle. And nothing happened, really. Night happened, just as the zoo had happened. In the dark, gathered around Marina's bed, we could see the zoo better than during the day; we saw that what we had felt watching the wolf was bottomless and unfathomable, and that we would never understand it, not then, not the next day, not in a year.

She'd never been so distant as she was then, so absent. At the zoo, it was not too late to have said, "We know who you are, Marina; we know your father died in the accident and your mother in the hospital. We know you're sad and we know you love us."

But at that moment we had to decide who Marina was to us. The one who invited us to her bed. Our hands and feet were cold. But she was still hot, as if she'd been locked up in the infirmary with just-baked bricks for a long time and was now giving off their stored heat. "The game is easy, and it lasts for days, because every day a different one of us is the game and every day it's different."

The room was still dark but we could hear her voice, boundless as the horizon. We know now, that we were brave that night, but we didn't know it then. We know now, too, that we didn't have to go to her, didn't have to get out of our beds, didn't have to feel the cold of the floor tiles, that it would have been easy to take her violence and her magnetism in our hand and crush it. And yet we went.

"It's easy," she repeated. Then she picked up her pillow to reveal blush, eyeliner, lipstick. "Each night, one of you is the doll. I put on her makeup, and she's the doll. And the rest of us look at her and play with her. She'll be a good dolly, and we'll be good to her."

"Where did you get that, Marina?"

73

"In the infirmary. The teacher left her purse there and I took it."

Finally someone turned on a light and we saw the expression on her face.

A tiny light, hidden under the sheets so we wouldn't get caught. We're supposed to forget everything, forget it all, pretend it never existed, but the way Marina looked when she taught us the game, that's something we have to hold on to: a cherished object.

"The doll has to be quiet; she's not allowed to talk. And she has to be very pale and sweet and wear this dress. She's like us, but in doll version; she can't live without us."

The differences between them diminished: from now on they were doll necks, doll hands, doll eyes and lips.

"Every night we'll all get to play with the doll and kiss her and tell her secrets. And she'll just look at us and listen to us, because she loves us, and we love her, too."

Suddenly she was spent, clammy. She struggled to speak, as if the idea of the game overwhelmed her.

"And every night when we go to sleep, we won't go to sleep. We'll dress the doll in the doll dress and put makeup on her and play with her. That's the way it's going to be."

That's the way it had to be.

That's the way it would be.

At first our eyes would slip in the night, until they adapted to the darkness. We almost couldn't see the sides of the dressers where our names were written. Slowly, we'd forget the cares of the day. We'd forget our times tables and spelling rules, forget the smell and taste of that night's dinner. Everything would be slow and amber-colored, like stuffy air in a closed-up room. But even if we really wanted to, we'd never rush. Feeling the contact of our nightgowns and the touch of our sheets, we'd pretend to be asleep, as if we'd been flooded by fatigue all of a sudden. Closing our eyes, we'd compel our bodies to produce the sleep-smell that convinced the adult it was okay for her to go. And we'd lie there like that, motionless, for several minutes. Then, in the dark of night, a strange sound would send the first sign. We'd billow, like skirts in the wind. We'd start to live inside the game, the anxiety of the game. Soon the second sign would come; there would be no doubt now. It could be anything: a whistle, the sound of creaking wood, even silence. And then slowly, we'd get out of bed, without even brushing up against each other, and our bodies would feel lighter. Not even then would we feel the cold of the floor tiles, be afraid of the dark. We *were* the cold, the dark. And so we'd go to Marina's bed, sleepwalkers, obsessed with one idea: starting the game.

Once we'd gathered around her bed, Marina would finally rise up and someone would turn on a light and put it under the sheets. We'd see her face, and for a moment she'd seem to hesitate. And then she'd say:

"You."

No more waiting. She'd just say:

"You."

Our last tie to the day, to the orphanage, would break

then. To us, that was when the doll's girl-life ended; an expression of fear, of pain, would cross her face. And when Marina signaled, we'd start to undress the chosen girl, thinking trivial thoughts: that we'd never noticed that mole on her shoulder before, that her face leaned comically to one side, that her nightgown had Donald Duck on it and was frayed at the hem. But as we undressed her, the chosen girl would become smaller, and more compact. She'd lose her smell. That precious, fragile thing, her smell, yes, even that would disappear. Her skin would become coarser, and so would our touch; everything would get a little rougher, a little tougher. To hide our uneasiness we'd make faces, tell jokes. Someone would even sing:

Minne Minnehaha went to see her Papa,
Papa died, Minne cried,
Minne had a newborn baby,
Stuck it in the bathtub to see if it could swim.

Almost in a whisper, so you could hardly hear it, so you didn't think about the doll's tiny body.

"You have to take off all of her clothes."

"Even her underwear?"

"Even her underwear. And then you have to put this dress on her, because this is the doll's dress."

The dress would be blue, and coarse, and no one would ever know where Marina had gotten it from. It would have a red cat playing with a green ball of yarn embroidered on the front. We would each touch the dress before putting it on the doll, as if we needed to prove that it was real, at least as real as the body of the doll who, now naked, would be waiting. There would be, truth be told, tremendous mistrust. The doll would wait, motionless. Once she was naked Marina would say:

"Now you have to dress her."

She'd make a very unhappy face. Her expression would go to pieces in one second. And we'd have to be very aware in that second because that was when we'd discover who the doll really was.

That was something we learned immediately: no two dolls were ever the same.

That was the way it had to be.

Some would be heavy and formless, as if constantly searching for a shape that never came, painful, chubby dolls with no message, and no one knew what to do with their spent flesh; others would be as taut as bows, marionettes with wide-open eyes, guilty as criminals; others would be fragile and delicate and we couldn't do anything to rid them of their delicacy; others would be born dead, impossibly cheap, one arm or leg longer than the other, or hair too coarse, or feet too dirty. Marina would always wait to see them before she put on their makeup.

Still naked, motionless, even before we put her dress on, the doll would await her face. That was when the game's second door would open, the scary one because who knew what was behind that closed door. It was always frightening there. You feared a terrible adventure. And what's to come is unnerving.

You close your eyes.

Then it's like you're dreaming.

Actually, you feel like you're on the verge of entering a dream but then don't, and then after a while all that's left is that feeling. Then even that fades, and a milky light seeps in through the crack, an anxiety that knows no words, no objects. But when you open your eyes, you see Marina's face putting on the makeup, bringing your hidden face to the surface. A frightened face. Very slowly, she twists the lipstick up and applies it to the doll's face. Your lips surrender to the color. Lips that had been so pale, almost transparent in the muted light, grow full, as if filling with blood.

Slowly your limbs sink into a warm sludge. You see the other girls' faces as if they'd just suddenly appeared out of nowhere. And then your eyes begin to feel tired.

"Close your eyes."

You close your eyes. You fall. It's as if you were wearing a mask. You feel the black pencil lining your eyes, emphasizing them. No one speaks, but you know exactly where each girl is and what she feels, and that wind is still blowing in from the window and that it's cold; you feel the scratchiness of the dress on your skin like a sack, and you love that contact, the presence, the feel of black eyeliner gliding across your eyelids. Marina pulls back a little, admiring her work. Then, calmly, she says:

"Now you're a doll."

And now you're a doll.

Suddenly, just like that, you're a doll.

You are passed from one set of hands to the next, from one bed to the next. You're never alone again. Safe inside the doll you love harder, feel deeper, exist boundlessly, no moderation. And yet you disregard the sound of girls kissing your cheek. Nothing matters now.

You have to let your arms flop at your sides so the girl will hold them up. You're frozen there, motionless, skin moist from a warm kiss that means nothing. Then you feel the yanking on your dress, greedy hands. The easiest thing is just to think you're going to die. But that thought, to a doll, has no meaning either. You feel it, but in no way does it stir you. Your eyes slowly drain of color until they're completely vacant. Your temperature drops, your heartbeat slows. You're not outside of anything, you're inside it; that's why they can leave their secrets with you. They inch their lips closer to your ear and whisper.

"Dolly, I . . ."

And the doll stiffens, excited, because even if you're not allowed to tell, you know the secret now.

Sad-armed doll, blue-dress doll, poor fallen thing that knows secrets.

FEAR WAS CONTAINED by the night. Fear was nocturnal, and it lied. It lied, again and again. And the dolls lived off of the fear they inhaled at night; they gorged on fear until at last something finally drove them back to bed and there they lay, spent. So slow, so patient.

Then in the morning they put on clean clothes and they were made new. Marina watched them sitting in class. It didn't seem possible that these girls were the same as those, and yet their faces were the same. There was one thing, though, that changed in the daytime: the rancor, the violence. A pent-up violence, flushed and physical. It came from the gut, from the gut of the clown with a chalkboard in his stomach, the clown that stood beside the teacher's desk. It was as if someone had written: "Now hate Marina" and they'd all obeyed.

But at night the game continued. And it revolved around Marina. When the lights went out she heard the dolls stir, come to life, come to her. Then, for a fleeting moment, that flash of power, of joy:

"You."

Why was it so different during the daytime? It was as though waking up flooded them with shame, and shame provoked rancor. They'd walk down to the bathroom, barefoot, and while they undressed before their showers, sometimes one of them would hit Marina. If she turned around, she'd see a cold face, sharp in the bright morning light, an accusatory face that suddenly made her want to ask forgiveness, a face that swelled and then shrank back to normal, to its composed daytime expression. And she couldn't say:

"It was her."

They were all close enough to have done it; all of their eyes glinted. And so daytime life began troublingly, so different from nighttime life. The orphanage came to life like an anthill in the sun. All of the game's gentleness was gone; there was only incomprehensible hostility. Inexplicably, the girls became veiled, difficult creatures once more. They ate breakfast, and their cheeks puffed with milk and cereal and they looked like they were gobbling up wounded flowers. They went to class and their rancor was there, too, in their silence. If Marina asked one of them to borrow a pencil or an eraser, they ignored her completely, and it seemed that their daytime hatred was the inverse of their nocturnal love; it felt like she'd regressed, felt worse, like she'd done something wrong and unforgiveable and irreversible. Suddenly she'd be overcome with leadenness, as if she'd reached out to them too urgently. But having put eyeliner and lipstick on almost each of their faces gave Marina a sense of serenity, a new level of intimacy. Each of those faces that had once been scattered and careless, each eye that was unmoving and sad, had stopped being a mistake. Now she perceived those faces as if, solely because of the game, they had suddenly become girl faces. Lazy, tired, hesitant, violent, Marina knew that the girls felt a love for her that was reserved for the night, for the game, and that was how she protected herself from their daytime rancor.

Sometimes it wasn't easy. One morning she saw that someone had written "BITCH" on her desk.

She had to rub it and rub it with spit until the letters began to disappear, forming little black pearls. She looked up, anguished, her face frozen like a scared rabbit, lips cold and hard, and no one responded. Then, slowly, her body seemed to swell with the word, and the word permeated everything: her dress, the classroom, the adult's eyes. The word soared up and then slammed into the class windows, unable to escape.

When night fell, she had already decided that she'd never play the game again. Hiding beneath the sheets, she lay there sticking out her tongue, licking her shoulder. Her feet cold, hard as a kernel of corn, she said to herself, "I'm never playing again."

And yet that very night, she played. The signals were sent and one by one the dolls got up. It was as though each one carried a fragile gift, a delicate gift inside her. She tried to breathe quietly so the dolls would think she was asleep, but they wouldn't go away. The weight of their bodies on her bed became awkward; each time a new body arrived, the springs creaked and "shhh" went from one to the next.

"I don't want to play," she said.

The dolls lifted the sheet.

"Aren't we going to play, Marina?"

"No."

Their faces were more fragile than ever. Soft love permeated everything, painstaking love, self-contained in its secrecy. What good would it have done to say, "I don't want to play because you wrote 'BITCH' on my desk"? The word no longer expressed any truth. The coming of the dolls' nighttime demeanor turned the word convex, perforated it; it no longer filled space but emptied it, like a sink when you pull the plug.

"Can't we play?"

"Okay."

Sometimes violence burst into the game, as if through a crack, and Marina was afraid to begin. But she'd arm herself with courage and say, randomly:

"You."

The sky capsized, falling down to the floor; everything was suspended except the doll. Touch began with nakedness. In a flash they brought her dress and she pulled it over the doll's soft body.

Only the game remained. Only the game was slow and puzzling. It was important to remain solemn, to let all ideas filter through the game. So one day she stole a knife from the dining room, and when nighttime came, she said, "Now we have to use the sacred knife to see the doll's blood."

As soon as she said it she knew that the words were bigger than the desire, knew that the two didn't match at all.

"The doll has to bleed," she said gravely.

She was pretty, too. She wore glasses. Her face was clean and unreadable, tiny, like a newborn animal. Though the doll lay motionless, Marina felt her body tense. The doll's rough skin registered cold: goosebumpy doll.

"It's very important."

She rested the knife on her leg. The doll quivered and then flinched. She cried one round, heavy tear. She whimpered.

"Ay!"

"You not allowed to talk; you're a doll."

Her blood flowed immediately and Marina put her finger on it. The doll paled.

"Now give the doll a glass of water; she's thirsty. One of you go get her a glass of water."

No one moved.

"I command you."

But they were rooted to the spot, paralyzed. The doll bled; the doll was absurd. They felt like crying; they felt ashamed to be alive.

"Fine then, I'll go."

And trembling with pride, she walked to the bathroom, filled a glass with water and returned, stepping carefully so as not to spill a drop. On the way back she stopped to spit in the glass. Not for vengeance, not from rage. She spit in the glass to preserve her own power, and she stood there for a moment, staring at her saliva in the water that the doll was about to drink.

"Give her the water," she ordered.

The doll drank slowly and then fainted, ashen. She fell onto her side and hit her head on one of the beds. Together, they carried her back to her own bed and pulled the covers up over her.

Marina felt exhausted and emotional that night, as if she'd been punished.

THEY SHAMED US. They said, "Look."

They put a name on everything.

They said, "Look what you did."

The names scared us. How is it that a thing gets caught inside a name and then never comes out again? Everything becomes bigger when it's named, but we didn't know that then; that was why we played. And we said, "Isn't this a good game."

We were all lovers and the game was our love.

We saw the letters of our names on the drawers; we imagined a doll like a color, living and glowing like a color. Then they said, "Look." The doll had turned evil; we didn't know what to do with her anymore. But the doll was pretty, too. She said, "Drink me, eat me." For a second, the doll was pretty; she tried her best to love. But instead of giving in to her all the time, we had to make her wait, until urgency became part of what she wanted to express. She would plead again, "Drink me, eat me." Where did the doll learn those words? And, when we didn't answer her, she'd grow calm again.

And so the days.

And afternoons.

She'd lie in the grass and pass the time braiding it. While we jumped rope, she'd play that weird, stupid game all by herself. It was so stupid, braiding blades of grass. But there she was, absorbed, prickly, as if she only had fifteen minutes to braid the whole entire lawn. Then we'd find her braids and yank them up. We'd say, "Look, Marina, your braid." This was her look: serious, focused, as if it were the only response possible. She'd just sit there, quiet. And then, in an almost friendly tone, she'd whisper, "Yes."

Sometimes she'd blank out, as if she suddenly forgot we were all there standing around her, as if she had no idea we were still there. She seemed to unfold, like crepe paper, like very thin cloth.

But when she came out of it the urgency would be back. "Drink me, eat me," and there was no name for what we wanted. And one day, she said:

"Tonight I'm going to be the doll."

"You can't, Marina."

"Why not?"

"Because."

"But I want to."

"But you can't, you're not allowed."

Then her lips became supplicant, contracting in a dark twitch. We were still one step away from that expression then; we were afraid to touch it.

"But I'm the one who made it up."

"That doesn't matter."

But by then she'd already started to look like a doll. She got closer each day.

"But I want to."

"But you can't, you're not allowed."

It was in her nature to be excluded. When the game was over she'd sit in the sun and close her eyes. Becoming unrecognizable to herself, inhaling happiness. She took breaks from us, too; sometimes she managed to forget about us, and then woke and returned to where we played, pretending not to have been watching her. We felt a dark pleasure in our bodies, a mixture of strength and fatigue. We longed for the moment she'd return.

"But I want to be the doll, too."

She knew that if she kept insisting she'd eventually get what she wanted, that the time would come when we could no longer stop her. She'd appear, transformed, new: her hands, her feet, her head, her body tense and slightly hunched over. And there would be no more humility, no entreaty in her voice, like when someone discovers something terrible within them and feels no fear, no shame, only arrogance.

She was swinging from the iron arch by the black statue and suddenly her whole body went taut. There she was now, aggressive. She leapt from the arch into our midst. She shouted.

"Look!"

We didn't dare to look up yet.

"Look at me, you big dummies!"

Then there was a long silence and we knew that it would be that very night. We clenched our teeth; our fear could keep us going for days and days. But nothing had happened yet, even after all that; there was just the chaos of laughter, greetings, shouting, words being formed. Her scheming eyes were hooded, her brows low, her face suddenly miniscule, ears huge, like a humble dog.

Yes, that was what we were waiting for, the doll's crude, tiny body. Night fell seamlessly. It was night over all of us. The adult would come and turn out the lights any minute. Secret things seemed to unite the two of them, Marina and the night.

First came an almost inaudible whisper. Then the voice rose up sweetly in the darkness. And it was as if we were hearing the song for the first time, as if it had just reached us for the first time, that song, never before sung by anyone.

Minne Minnehaha went to see her Papa,
Papa died, Minne cried,
Minne had a newborn baby,

Stuck it in the bathtub to see if it could swim.

Yes, and then we knew exactly where the doll's body was, there where the darkness and the sound met.

Now she was still, waiting. For the first time she left herself open, her face open to our curiosity. Her little eyebrows. Her open eyes. The tender seclusion of her lips. The fine hairs, like peach fuzz, on the nape of her neck. Her hair, darker now, softer. The fascination of her fine hair, the fascination of imagining Marina's hair like a microscopic forest that we could enter if we were the size of a mosquito. The fascination of our secrets, the secrets we were about to tell her because she was so close now, and she loved us. We saw up close now what we'd admired from afar for so many months: the curve of her ear; the slight shine on the flesh of her eyelid; her nostrils; the smooth skin on her neck that sloped and became rougher as it reached her shoulder; the contour of her shoulder bones.

"We have to take off her nightgown."

"Her underwear, too?"

"Her underwear, too."

She shivered, and suddenly, there before us, lay her body. We felt tender towards her arms and legs, the tenderness you feel for things too fragile, precious toys you have to touch carefully; we didn't know how to feel about her torso, two contradictory feelings pulled us in opposite directions. You could hardly see her scar, and there was a small hollow below her chest and above her stomach. We thought it was pretty.

"That's pretty," we said, and Marina's face relaxed, just for a second. She leaned her head back, her eyelids almost closed; suddenly she blossomed, smiling, delighted.

Dolly, once I peed in my pants in class and when everybody found out I wanted to die, and I thought over and over and over again: I wish I was dead right now.

For a few minutes nothing on her face was still. Eyes and lips and nose and mouth were all there, but not connected; you had to really stare at her to remember that she was pretty and that we liked her. It started on her skin, on the surface of her skin. As if there were many layers, one on top of the other, and suddenly she was rough to the touch. We touched her and we couldn't understand what was happening: suddenly she was far away, but without having gone anywhere, still here: something impossible that only happens in books and movies.

Dolly, sometimes I get under the covers and say bitch, whore, cunt, fuck, dick.

Then very very gently, she closed her eyes, and we watched her eyeballs dart behind her eyelids. Where before there had been eyes, now there was very fine skin, closed, silent, trapped by an eyelid that you could touch with your finger, and when you touched it, it twitched, a tiny shudder, and her eyebrows crinkled up; it was like a baby summer, and inside it, a sun, all in miniature. We always liked little things.

Dolly, one time I saw the devil in a dream and he came up to me and ate my legs, and then I didn't have any legs.

Yes, always little things. And then we were discovering that her body was smaller than it had ever been. And with the smallness came fascination. Because anything small fits in our hand, and we can touch it, and move it, and guess what it's for, and see how it works. Someone took the doll's hand and made her hit herself. A silly game that the doll accepted, because she was a doll and dolls accept everything. Because dolls are dried up and empty, and they hardly speak, and their bodies are heavy with sleep and they're silly.

Dolly, when you first got here I wanted to be like you, and I watched you, and one day I came up to you and I thought: if I touch her dress, I'll be like her. And then I touched you and nothing happened.

But the doll resisted; we moved her hand and just when she was about to hit her face, she'd push back a little, so she didn't hit it as hard. Then, after doing it several times, she opened her eyes and said firmly:

"Stop it."

"You can't talk; you're a doll."

For three seconds the doll was alive, then she closed back in on herself, as if she'd finally accepted the game; and everything else, everything we'd done up until then, was just the beginning. She closed her eyes again.

Dolly, sometimes I say: My mother is a whore; she left me.

What happened next? The game was not right, suddenly. As if something had broken, and nothing was simple anymore: not the game, not us. We started putting makeup on her face. We gave her a huge mouth, enormous eyes. Because her mouth had to be like that, all red, and her eyes all black, and we pressed hard, entranced by the way the pencil bore into her skin, the way the lipstick went almost up to her cheeks. We inhaled the lipstick smell, sweet and sticky, as if the doll had burst, like liquid in a filled chocolate, like liquid that was red and we could eat it.

Dolly, one time I hit you and I was scared, because I didn't know how I felt.

We started jostling against each other, as if we were in each other's way, but without knowing why. It was as though we'd suddenly gotten hungry, as if it were lunchtime and they'd said we were having fried ham and cheese, and we were overeager. Ears pricked up, hands tense, a feeling bigger than us enveloped the room, the beds, the dressers with our names written on the drawers in colors. We didn't know whether or not to laugh. We were happy. We joined hands and started to circle around the doll.

Dolly, I'm filled with shame.

The doll opened one eye, her right one, slowly, surprised. Her hands were still, resting on her knees, waiting, for what she did not know. We didn't know either. It was just the momentum of the circle, the knowledge that something was about to spring like a coil, the conviction that the circle would spin faster and faster and faster until it was so fast that it would vanish into the air, and we'd vanish with it, everything would vanish.

Dolly, I broke off your hands and legs and I buried you out with the caterpillars.

Who leapt first? Was it me? Was it you? Who flew from the circle through the stale air separating us from the doll? Who pounced first? Then all we felt was fury. Passed from arm to arm, from mouth to mouth, nothing but spit and fury. Yes. That thing we couldn't understand, that thing that we wanted and loved, smooth pink fingernails, someone must have covered the doll's mouth so she wouldn't scream. Was that me? Was it you? Someone must have pushed her because we all fell to the floor, on top of her. Someone must have held her down so she'd stop kicking and be still, stiller than any other doll had ever been, so still that we had to get our breath back.

Dolly, I cried for days, and I missed you.

We played with her all night, so still.

Then, overflowing with gratitude and joy, we sat around her and slowly kissed her lips one by one, as if we were eating.

Translator's Note

Lisa Dillman

One of the first things that struck me when I read *Such Small Hands* was the way in which Andrés Barba, at the time in his early thirties, managed to render so stunningly, poignantly, and convincingly the voices of orphaned girls, to recreate, almost hermetically, their thoughts and inse-curities—their suffocating world. Here he was, a grown man, plunging readers into the complex psychology of a group of seven-year-old girls. It left me astounded. In the eight years since the book's Spanish publication, Barba has continued to write many more masterful novels and novellas, and I'm no longer shocked by his talent. I've simply come to expect it. His books delve vertiginously into the mindset of characters who are on the verge of change—struggling to reconcile two (or more) contrasting perspectives, two (or more) disparate social realities, two (or more) seemingly incompatible ways of existing in the world.

In 2009, after tracking down Barba's email address, I proposed translating the novel to him. I spent many months drafting an initial version of the manuscript and then traveled to Madrid to meet him in person and ask countless questions about his choice of verb tense and mode, his idiosyncratic punctuation, surreal images, and haunting atmosphere. At the time I was so nervous that I pretended—to date I've never told him this—that I was going to be in Madrid to visit friends and thus could conveniently meet him while there. In truth, I went explicitly to meet Barba, and took advantage of the fact that one of my best friends happened to live there, too. (¡Mil gracias, Alejandro!) Barba's generosity and openness were, and continue to be, remarkable. Before we'd even met, he offered me a place to stay, as well as his time and insight. Over the course of subsequent Andrés Barba novels that I've now translated, I have benefited again and again from his generosity and frankness and continue to feel indebted to him. A renowned translator himself (of Melville, Conrad, and Henry James, to name a few), he understands the issues involved that many writers don't. He knows, for instance, that the sound of a sentence, its intrinsic rhythms and cadence, matter just as much as the meaning of the words in it. He knows that being "faithful"—a problematic word for many reasons—to an original often does not equate to using English dictionary equivalents, because semantics is one element of many that goes into creating the mood and tone that are representative of any given book. Barba's vast translation experience, therefore, makes his perspective refreshing and liberating when we discuss approaches and dilemmas.

Translation is the closest form of reading there can be: by its very nature, it's a process that requires you to examine and reflect on every word of a text both in isolation and in relationship to those surrounding it—it's *con*-text, the text that is with it. But in addition, of course, translation is a term often used metaphorically. The word itself, from the Latin *translatio*, means *to carry across*, and this is a process that occurs in many realms. Indeed, there is, for example, an entire field of translational medicine, which examines how medical knowledge and scientific advancement are carried out, brought "from bench to bedside," as the expression goes. In this metaphorical light, it's fair to say that *Such Small Hands* is in many ways about translation. The novel centers around Marina and a group of girls at an orphanage who are struggling with all sorts of emotions that they don't know how to make sense of, how to handle, or what to do with. Love, desire, envy, and jealousy are not things they are equipped to discuss. So their emotions are translated into actions, sometimes touching and sweet, sometimes cruel, even violent. In his finely wrought prose, Barba allows us to see through them, to apprehend the reasons for their behavior. He translates the girls into language we feel on a gut level. And this is translation's job, at its core: to carry across, to *make* sense.

Such Small Hands is one of the most meaningful books of my life: it is not only the first of the five novels by Andrés Barba that I've translated but also the only book that I have ever translated on spec. I had no contract, no prior interest expressed from publishers and no funding for the project. And yet so taken was I by the novel—its plot, the rendering of mood, the languorous prose and astonishing crystalline intensity of emotion, the granular visual descriptions (Oh, the caterpillars! Oh, the car seat!), which are infused with nail-biting tension—that I decided to undertake the project anyway. This is something that most translators advise against. There are too many stories of heartbreak out there: sometimes the pined-for book is picked up by a publisher who then has it translated by someone else; more often, completed translation manuscripts end up in a drawer and never see the light of day.

For all of these reasons, I can hardly express my joy at the fact that, all these years later, the newly launched Transit Books has published this remarkable novel as its first translation. I'm so grateful to Andrés for having written it, and indescribably grateful to Adam and Ashley for having been so taken with it.

—Decatur, GA, August 2016

Afterword

Edmund White

Every once in a while a novel does not record reality but creates a whole new reality, one that casts a light on our darkest feelings. Kafka did that. Bruno Schulz did that. Now the Spanish writer Andrés Barba has done it with the terrifying *Such Small Hands*, which introduces us to the psychosis of childhood emotions and midnight rituals. This is a unique book.

It is reputedly based on an incident that occurred in Brazil in the 1960s, in which the girls at an orphanage took the life of another child and played with her body parts for a week. But *Such Small Hands* is not a grisly *fait divers*. Following the lead of Jean Genet, who in *The Maids* turned a newspaper account of two psychopathic servants killing their mistress into a strangely hieratic, ritualistic tragedy, Barba has subsumed the *grand guignol* aspects of the bloody anecdote into a poetic meditation on love and childhood.

To signal that he doesn't intend for his novel to be just a psychological study of little Marina, unable to express her grief after her parents' death, Barba has introduced a Greek chorus of the other orphans. They are all in love with her; her introduction into the orphanage has changed their lives. She is beautiful and small and delicate. She has a mysterious scar on her shoulder caused by the same car accident that killed her parents; it seems almost like the scar where an angel wing was removed. The orphans are fascinated by Marina who, after all, lived a normal middle-class life with indulgent parents until recently; she has only lately joined their ranks and become orphaned.

Everything she does steals their attention. For instance, for a while she stops eating, repulsed by the sight of other girls stuffing their mouth holes. She seems somehow purer and stronger because of her fasting.

Then she invents a game in which each night, after lights out, Marina chooses a new girl to play the doll— passive, silent, asleep, motionless. Each "doll" is stripped of all her clothes and dressed in a special scratchy outfit. The girls are nearly hypnotized by this game, perhaps because it appeals to everyone's fear (and forbidden wish) to be turned into an object, without a will or even motility, the unconscious target of everyone's attention, utterly without responsibility for one's actions (since one has none). Marina seems to understand the appeal of the game she has devised; she hints that she will be introducing a game hours before she reveals its exact rules and builds up enormous suspense and curiosity.

> "Tonight we're going to play a game," she said.
> "What game, Marina?"
> "Just a game I know."
> "How do you play?"
> "I'll tell you tonight."
> "Can't you tell us now?"
> "No. Tonight."

Ever since her parents' death Marina has been playing with a doll given to her by a psychologist, perhaps for companionship, perhaps as a means of externalizing her bottled-up grief. The other girls, torn between their desire to love Marina and to hurt her, steal her doll and return it only limb by limb, in a terrible prefiguring of the catastrophe of this drama.

Although *Such Small Hands* is constructed around a plot that has all the inevitability and dignified horror of a Sophoclean tragedy, we read it with intense pleasure not just for its trajectory but for the ingenuity of its prose. As we submit to its murmuring cadences we thrill with the recognition not of familiar, ready-to-hand feelings but of long-forgotten ones. The psychologist Jean Piaget posited that children pass through stages of cognitive development that radically affect our perceptions of the world; if we could suddenly enter the consciousness of a child we would understand nothing since a child's mental life is organized by entirely different schemas than those used by an adult.

Barba is not a scientist and his book is not the demonstration of a theory, but when we read a paragraph like this one about a dormitory of sleeping girls we are convinced that we are plunged into an archaic system of perception that we've forgotten but that is oddly reminiscent:

> All together, they looked like a team of sleepy little horses. Something in their faces slackened, became friendly. They slept with an unbearable patience. When they were asleep they were like an oil painting, they gave Marina the impression that different faces rose up from beneath their faces, faces that bore no resemblance to their daytime voices: peculiar, polished faces. They had a defiant, challenging quality about them despite being at rest, like dozing predators.

This roiling, unstable perception of the surround reveals the almost psychotic, oneiric processes of a child's mind that has not yet been able to understand the notion of object constancy, that doesn't realize that there are things out there that remain the same no matter how they are illuminated by our imagination. Everything for a child is in flux, dangerously so, and Barba captures perfectly this seasickness, this instability.

When the girls cluster around Marina's bed to play the dolly game, the chorus says:

> How did our desire begin? We don't know. Everything was silent in our desire, like acrobats in motion, like tightrope walkers. Desire was a big knife and we were the handle.

Anyone who has ever fallen asleep during a lecture knows that the mind instantly starts producing images as one is half aware of the setting and the speech, little cartoons that try to make sense of the waking and sleeping realities. This is the unmoored, precarious image-making of Barba's girls. They can't explain what they're feeling nor why, they can only paddle in this ghastly fluid between reality and fantasy. Barba has returned us to the nightmare of childhood.

ANDRÉS BARBA first became known in 2001 when his novel *La hermana de Katia*, shortlisted for the Herralde Prize, was published to considerable public and critical acclaim. It was followed by *Ahora tocad música de baile, Versiones de Teresa*, winner of the Torrente Ballester award, and *Agosto, octubre, Muerte de un caballo*, for which he won the 2011 Juan March short novel award, *Ha dejado de llover*, and his latest work, *En presencia de un payaso*. His books have been translated into ten languages.

LISA DILLMAN translates from Spanish and Catalan and teaches in the Department of Spanish and Portuguese at Emory University. Some of her recent translations include *Signs Preceding the End of the World*, by Yuri Herrera, which won the 2016 Best Translated Book Award; *Rain Over Madrid* and *August, October*, by Andrés Barba; *Monastery*, co-translated with Daniel Hahn, by Eduardo Halfon; and *Salting the Wound*, by Víctor del Árbol.

Transit Books is a nonprofit publisher of international and American literature, based in Oakland, California. Founded in 2015, Transit Books is committed to the discovery and promotion of enduring works that carry readers across borders and communities. Visit us online to learn more about our forthcoming titles, events, and opportunities to support our mission.

TRANSITBOOKS.ORG